Love Possessed

A Crimson Moon Hideaway Novel

I0529624

USA Today Bestselling Author

Cassidy K. O'Connor

Table of Contents

Chapter One

Chapter Two

Chapter Three

Chapter Four

Chapter Five

Chapter Six

Chapter Seven

Chapter Eight

Chapter Nine

Epilogue

ABOUT THE AUTHOR

~Other Books by the Author~

Chapter One

Raine Shadowglow loved love. As a cupid, it was in their genetic code to make it the sole focus of their lives. Too bad for him. He sucked at being a cupid and if he didn't get his shit together soon, he was going to be out of a job and a disgrace to his family.

He'd never been to the Cupid Expo or the resort that hosted the event. Crimson Moon Hideaway was supposed to be the premier destination for paranormals and supernaturals of all kinds to go relax and be themselves. He wasn't going there for vacation though. The Cupid Council ordered him to attend the expo.

He hadn't been a cupid long, but his success rate was barely thirty percent. There wasn't another cupid that he knew of with less than a ninety percent.

He didn't know what the problem was. He practiced his archery skills every day and always hit his assigned targets, but for some reason, the couple would separate within days.

This was his last chance to learn from the best and figure out why he sucked so bad.

He hopped out of the cab before the valet even had the door open.

"Welcome to Crimson Moon Hideaway. Head inside to the registration area and we'll meet you there with your luggage."

Raine held his hand up as he shook his head. "It's okay. I just have this one bag. I'm only here a couple of days."

"Of course, sir. Have a pleasant stay." The blond surfer-looking guy rushed off to help the next car in line.

The tiny heart on Raine's wrist that told him when another cupid was nearby lightly pulsed.

Hopefully, the council had some way to pause that this weekend or his wrist was going to go numb from all the cupids in the area.

The hotel had taken the Valentine and cupid theme to a whole new level. The lobby was covered in flowers and hearts. It was impressively tasteful, not like something you would see at a middle school dance.

"Next."

Raine's mouth went dry. The gorgeous woman behind the counter had a distinct glow that could only mean she was an angel. "Um, hello ma'am. I'm checking in."

"Of course, I just need your I.D."

He handed her his license and glanced around, trying not to stare at her.

"I have you on the fifth floor, room 519. I see you are here with the Cupid Expo group. They have a check-in area on the second floor near the conference rooms. Here's a packet with everything there is to see and do at the resort. I hope you enjoy your stay."

Raine made his way across the large seating

area around the fireplace. He loved seeing all the different types of paranormals hanging out and talking. He got on the elevator with a young couple who were so busy kissing they barely noticed when he got off on the second floor.

He found the check-in table for the expo and gave his name. The older man rifled through a stack of folders and handed him one with his name on it. "We get started bright and early tomorrow, so don't be late."

For a cupid, the man wasn't very jovial.

Raine got back in the elevator and took it up to his room.

The view from his window was incredible. The redwood trees stood taller than the hotel, but even on the fifth floor, it was hard to grasp the sheer size of the trees. He loved the outdoors and since the expo didn't start until the next morning, he had plenty of time to explore.

He tossed his bag on the bed and thumbed through the packet he'd gotten at check-in. "A zip-line cool." He'd never done it before and this one somehow took you up to the top of a mountain. Based on the map, he'd be able to hike back down and back to the hotel just as it was getting dark.

He grabbed a water bottle out of the mini-fridge and took the elevator up to the roof.

The thinnest man Raine had ever seen was sitting on a stool by the zip line. If he didn't know better, he would swear he could see through him.

"Afternoon. Want to take a ride?"

"This will take me to the mountain and then I can hike back, right?"

"Absolutely." He held out the harness to help Raine. "The real question is how fast do you want to go? You can go the normal speed or I can send some nice air currents your way."

Now Raine understood why the man looked the way he did. "You're a sylph, right?"

"Indeed I am, Gavin's the name." He held out his thin hand.

"Raine, nice to meet you. I've never done this before so I'm thinking I want the normal speed this time. Maybe I'll take you up on that offer next time."

Once he was hooked into place, Gavin gave him a little wave and a gust of wind came from nowhere and sent him careening. He glanced down and saw the pool and lazy river before getting lost among the trees. When it looked like no one was around, he let out a shout. He hadn't felt so free since coming into his powers. It had been nothing but stress and anxiety. This was a release he didn't know he needed.

All too soon, the ride was over. A small redhead was waiting on the edge with a big smile. "Sounds like you enjoyed yourself."

His cheeks heated with embarrassment. "I didn't realize I was that loud."

She waved him off. "Please, everyone yells who does this."

He waited until she'd completely unhooked him before pulling out the small map of the grounds. "I'm not exactly the hearty outdoorsman type. How bad will it be to hike back to the resort?"

"Stick to the trail and you'll have no trouble. I'd say watch for animals but out here you never know what's wild and what's shifter."

He hadn't thought about that... "So don't just go up to a cute animal and think I can pet it, got it."

Her eyes rounded before she started laughing. "For a second there, I thought you might be serious. Enjoy your walk and if you aren't back by dark, I'll make sure to send a search party out."

The hike started out easy enough. The incline wasn't too hard to traverse. After a bit, the wind picked up. He cocked his head, listening carefully. It sounded like whispers being carried across the mountain. The sound was faint but persistent. He tried ignoring the incessant murmuring, but it felt like electricity was buzzing across his skin.

He really didn't want to leave the trail, but he couldn't stop himself. The brush got thicker the deeper he walked. A small cave came into view. The whispers were coming from inside.

This was how every horror movie started, but he was at Crimson Moon Hideaway. Merlin was here. No way would they let anything bad happen.

At the entrance, he took out his cell phone and turned on the flashlight. "This is the dumbest thing I've ever done." For a brief second, he considered turning back, but the whispers grew more insistent. "Ugh, fine. If I get eaten by a bear, I am going to be really pissed."

There wasn't much to look at, moss-covered walls, rocks scattered around, a dripping sound coming from somewhere. In the very back, along the wall, an odd shape stuck out among the shadows. As he got closer, it became clear it was a box. He kneeled down and touched it. The whispers instantly silenced. "Yeah, that's not creepy."

He lifted the box to get a better look at it. "Oh, fuck no. Screw this." It wasn't made of wood, it was crudely constructed out of bones. He set it down and jumped to his feet. The whispering echoed throughout the cave.

"Come on, really?" He paced until the noise got to be too much. "Fine, fine, I'll open it, but I swear to god nothing better jump out at me."

He sat down and laid the box on his lap. Taking a deep breath, he closed his eyes and threw the lid open. When nothing happened, he peeked one eye open than the other. Inside was a rock, or was it a fossilized egg? He held his flashlight close, trying to figure out what it was.

He twisted it side to side and saw nothing to hint at its contents. He sat the rock back in the box and put it back where it was. "I came, I saw it, and now I can go."

He turned to leave, and the whispers came back. "You win. I'll take the damn rock, but I'm leaving the creepy bone box."

If he told anyone this story, he'd definitely leave out the part where he talked to the disembodied voices.

He grabbed the egg and took off before the voices could yell at him again.

The forest was probably beautiful, but he didn't really remember. He rushed back to the resort so he could put the rock down. It felt warm, and his hand tingled. He just wanted to get rid of the thing.

He nodded to the cupid's he passed on the way to his room, hoping they wouldn't try to stop and talk.

He placed the egg on the coffee table and sat on the couch, staring at it. "Okay, now what?" He glanced around, expecting the voices to come back, but it was silent. Not knowing what else to do, he took a few pictures and sent them to friends who might know more than he did.

He grabbed the hotel phone and ordered dinner and pre-ordered breakfast. If he was going to play Indiana Jones, he was going to need a full stomach.

Out of the corner of his eye, the rock wiggled. When he spun his head toward it, the movement stopped. He looked away and saw it again and jerked his head back quickly, but it just sat there, not moving. "Some freaking dinosaur is going to hatch and I'll be responsible for people getting eaten."

He stared at the egg rock thing, daring it to move while he waited for his food. He wasn't going to let it surprise him.

Chapter Two

Raine forced his eyes open. He had passed out on the couch. He sat up and looked around, confused. A tray of breakfast foods was on the coffee table and he'd apparently eaten all of it. He didn't remember finishing dinner the night before, let alone sleeping, or answering the door to get the breakfast tray.

He grabbed his phone. It was morning, and he couldn't remember the night before. A text from a friend popped up.

Demetri: Sorry man, no idea what that thing is. Maybe a museum will buy it! I'll send it to Seraphine and see if she knows.

The egg rock thing. He totally forgot about it. He tossed his phone aside and searched the table. It was gone. He jumped up and heard a crunch. He lifted his foot and found gravel and dust covering the carpet. "Shit." The egg thing must have hatched.

His head spun from corner to corner, looking for something, anything, out of place. He searched under the bed and in the bathroom, nothing.

He peeked his head out into the hallway and didn't see blood or hear screaming. Maybe it had been empty.

The welcome address to kick off the expo was in less than an hour. He had to hurry so he wouldn't miss it.

He showered quickly and stood at the bathroom mirror, brushing his teeth.

Ugh, why can't you hear me?

Raine choked, sending toothpaste across the mirror. That voice was definitely in his head and definitely wasn't his. Was the egg thing inside him? What the fuck had he done?

Wait, you heard me, didn't you?

Dumbfounded, he nodded, but said nothing.

Finally, I've been trying to talk to you for hours. What year is it?

"Year? It's 2022."

I've been gone for two hundred years! Those cloth puppets.

His jaw fell open. "I'm sorry, we'll get back to the four hundred year thing, but first, what's a cloth puppet?"

Priests that hunt anything that isn't like them.

"Next question, how did you get in my head?" He was really trying hard not to freak out.

I guess my spirit was locked in something. You freed it, and you were the closest living object for me to inhabit? This is new for me too.

His cell phone chimed that the opening session was starting in fifteen minutes. "Look, I'm on thin ice here, and have something I gotta go do. If you can just hang tight for a little bit, we'll get back to your problem."

My lack of body is a serious problem. You can't leave me now.

His whole body exploded into waves of pins and needles. He grunted in pain and when he opened his eyes again, everything was very wrong. *Did you just take control of my body?*

She subconsciously tried brushing the hair from her shoulder, only to realize his head was bald. "I'm sorry, I didn't want to, but I need to figure out what happened to me so I can get out of you."

I told you I would help you, but if I don't get downstairs, I'm going to lose my whole purpose for living.

"That sounds dramatic. Just hang tight. I'll give you back control as soon as I can."

You can't do this, please!

She ignored his protests as she searched the dresser and grabbed clothes.

I can't go downstairs in sweatpants. Go to those doors over there and get one of my suits. And LET ME HAVE MY BODY BACK!

She grabbed the first suit hung up and got dressed. She held the tie up for a second, then tossed it aside.

She went to the hotel room door and pulled it open. "What? There's just more doors. How do I get outside?" His body jerked against the doorframe. He was fighting to get control back. "Stop it, I'm going to give you your body back... eventually."

An older couple paused in the hall, staring at him.

"Morning."

They rushed past him.

"That was rude. I wasn't going to eat them. Maybe they are leaving." She took off after them but froze when a set of doors slid open and they got on and the doors closed again. "What magic is that?"

That is an elevator. You've been gone a while. You aren't ready for this world. Let me take control.

She shook her head and pushed the button she'd seen the man press. She gingerly stepped onto the elevator, unsure of what to expect. For a few seconds, nothing happened, then it started moving.

"Ahhhh."

His body jerked against the wall as Raine got control back.

Fine, you win. Do what you need to do, then please help me.

Raine felt sorry for the woman, but he couldn't lose his job. "I promise. I want you out of my body just as much."

He leaned forward and hit the second floor button and smiled politely at the couple that got on at the third floor.

You could have told me what to do.

He ignored her. He needed her to panic, and she did.

"Have a nice day." He nodded to the couple as he got off.

He followed the stream of cupids toward the conference center.

"Raine, a moment, please."

"Shit." Raine pasted on a smile and walked over to the older cupid standing near the door. "Morning Ralph."

"I'm glad to see you here. The council is

expecting improvements after this. Pay attention to the seminars and learn everything you can. This is your last chance to improve."

The older man didn't wait for a response. He spun on his heel and went inside.

How dare he talk to you like that. Let's kill him.

Raine choked as he swallowed. He had to mumble quietly so people didn't think he was talking to himself. "We don't kill people. What kind of supernatural are you again?"

Um... an immortal.

Before he could question her further, Guthrie James walked to the podium and shooshed everyone. "Morning, welcome to the Cupid Expo 2022."

You're a cupid, that's hysterical. Where's your bow and arrow?

It was really annoying to hear her laugh in his head, but he pretended he didn't and focused on the councilman on stage.

Guthrie continued. "Who's ready for all things love?"

Bahahaha, this is hysterical.

"You're not a very nice person, are you?" He whispered under his breath. "Do you really want my help?"

I'm sorry, I'll try to be good.

He hadn't met many immortal beings, and now he was glad he hadn't.

Raine didn't answer as he tuned back into the speaker. "You have the schedules. There are three breakout sessions before lunch, then you can take advantage of one of the many restaurants the resort has to offer. After that, we have four more hours of breakouts. We hope you enjoy the lineup we've created for you."

The crowd clapped, then got up to disperse.

Raine studied the schedule and chose his first class.

Where are we going first?

He could hear the mirth in her voice still. He'd give anything not to answer her, but she was going to find out anyway. "We're going to 'How to arrange the perfect meet cute.'"

She snort laughed. *I don't know what a meet cute is, but this sounds great. Lead the way.*

This was going to be the longest day of his life.

Chapter Three

Raine's head was throbbing. They made it through the day with plenty of taunting and laughter in his head. When food was around the parasitic immortal in his head took control. She admitted to doing the same with dinner and breakfast that morning. It explained why he had no memory of the meals. She had a serious thing for food and ordered enough that he looked like a serious glutton. Thankfully, the waitress at Lumberjacks hadn't even batted an eye at his large order.

Your day is done. Can we go now, please?

Raine collapsed onto the bed in his room

and stared at the ceiling. "You know, I just realized I don't know your name and I figure I shouldn't call you a parasite."

She gasped in his head. *Well, that was rude. I didn't exactly choose your body either. To answer your question, though, my name is Ephra.*

"Okay, Ephra, did you have a plan?"

If you get me some blood, I might be able to contact people I used to know.

"Wait a second, there aren't many supes that use blood like that. Exactly what kind of immortal are you?" He dreaded what she was about to say.

There was silence for several seconds.

Don't freak out… I'm a demon.

"Shit." He jumped off the bed and paced the floor. "Okay, tell me what to do. I definitely want you out of my body immediately."

Hey, that's demon discrimination.

"So the priests that trapped you did so because you're evil."

I don't think it was their place to judge.

"Right, like you did nothing to deserve it."

If you aren't even going to listen to my side, then I won't bother you with it.

He could hear in her tone that he'd upset her. "I'm sorry, Ephra. I've never met a demon before and everything I know about your kind is not good." She stayed silent. "Other than blood, what can we do?"

Where do the nearest ley lines intersect? Maybe I can tap into that magic and contact someone.

"Ley lines? Like I have any clue." He grabbed his laptop and sat on the couch.

This is amazing. What do you call this?

"It's a computer, and this is the internet. I can pretty much search for anything and learn about it."

You have it so much better these days. Where does this internet say we should go?

He pulled up a map and pointed to where they were. "The resort is here. It looks like the magical strength varies by spot. There are a few not too far away."

Those are all the weaker ones. I'm going to need a lot of power.

"Okay, the closest strong lines intersect here in Yellowstone."

Great, let's go.

"Hang on." He searched the route from Crimson Moon to Yellowstone. "It's a fourteen hour drive. I can take you there after the expo is over, but we can't go tonight. I won't be back by morning."

Please, I know you want a demon out of you as much as I want out of you.

"You are so impatient for someone that is dependent on me. Hold on for another day and a half and I'll get you there."

As soon as the words were out, he knew what was going to happen. The pins and needles spread across his body as she took control. *Damn you Ephra.*

"I'm already damned, thank you very much."

She marched out of the room, wearily got on the elevator, and made it down to the lobby.

"Yo, Raine. Where you been hiding?"

"Who are these people?" Ephra whispered.

I guess you shouldn't just take over other people's bodies, should you?

The young guy walked up and slapped him on the back. "Dude, get your bathing suit on, grab a drink, and let's go hang at the pool."

The group with him all had drinks in hand and looked like they'd already had a few. "I don't have time for this."

She rushed past them and out the huge lobby doors.

You can't just be rude to my friends.

"When this is all over, you can explain it to them."

Ten steps out the door, a loud noise made her jump. A car slammed on their brakes and narrowly missed hitting her.

You are going to get me killed and then we'll both be screwed.

"What is that thing?"

"Sir, are you okay?"

A valet was standing in front of him. "Let's get you out of the lane." He led her back toward the door. "Do you need a car? Are you heading to town?"

Just go back inside Ephra, you're being ridiculous.

"I need to get to Yellowstone immediately."

"So I guess a car is out. Do you already have a plane ticket or you can use one of the portals on the property if you have that kind of magic?"

"Do we have that magic?"

Raine knew she was asking him, but the valet looked utterly confused. "Well, the hotel has a few spots where you can open a portal, but you have to have the magic to use it."

"Raine..."

He could hear the impatience in her voice.

The valet glanced at the sky. "I don't think it's supposed to rain. I heard it would be clear skies all weekend."

"This is absurd. Fine, you win." His body shook as she released control and let Raine take the lead. He glanced down at the guy's name tag. "I'm sorry Jared, I'm not feeling myself. Sorry I bothered you."

He spun around and went back into the hotel. "You're out of your element. Please let me get through this weekend and I'll get you settled."

I take it back, the future sucks.

"Come on, I'll buy you an ice cream."

Chapter Four

E phra had moaned so many times while eating the ice cream cone that everyone in the parlor was staring at them.

Ephra, you have got to quiet down.

He'd never admit it out loud, but her moans definitely had him feeling emotions other than embarrassment. Cupid's can't be attracted to demons though. There has to be some cosmic rule against it.

"This is so good. How do you not eat this for every meal?"

You get used to it.

"Raine, mind if I join you?"

Shit, Ephra give me back control.

They'd gotten better at switching. The change was barely noticeable. "Callie, I didn't know you were here."

The young blonde gave him a long hug. "It's been so long." She sat on the stool next to his and leaned forward so her breasts were grazing his forearm.

I know of ten ways we can kill her and dispose of the body without anyone finding her.

Rainc bit the inside of his cheek to keep from laughing.

"What are you up to these days?"

Her fingers traced small circles on the top of his hand. "Oh, you know, bouncing from here and there. I saw the expo was here this weekend and thought I'd see if you were here."

"This is my first time, so you got lucky."

Pfft.

"I love getting lucky." She winked at him. "It's freezing in here. Let's go sit outside for a bit."

He really didn't want to encourage her. "It's getting late,"

"No way. I'm not letting you get away." She grabbed his arm and yanked him up.

Just knock her down and make a run for it.

Ephra's jealousy was comical enough to put up with Callie for a bit longer.

He tossed the ice cream cone in the garbage can on the way out.

No, I wasn't done with that!

Thank goodness she couldn't see the evil smile on his face.

Callie led them to a set of loungers in an alcove. She whistled at a waiter before laying down.

A surfer looking guy walked up and smiled at them. "Evening, what can I get for you?"

Callie jumped in first. "Colin, sweetie, we'll have two of your Cupid's Arrow specials."

He nodded and walked away.

"And what's a Cupid's Arrow?" Not that he was surprised the resort had special drinks just for the expo.

"It's fruity and pink and has a cute little plastic bow and arrow sticking out of it. I've had quite a few over the last couple of days. If you get a chance, you should watch that guy behind the bar. He's an octopus shifter and when it's busy, he has multiple arms going at the same time and it's crazy to watch."

Colin returned, gave them their drinks, and they were on their own.

"It's been what, two years since the last time I saw you?"

He had to think back. She always seemed to pop up everywhere. "Yeah, it was Chicago, I think."

She tossed her hair back and laughed. "That's right. We had a few fun nights, didn't we?" Her fingers grazed up the side of his arm.

Harlot.

Raine hadn't heard anyone called that in decades.

Callie stood up and straddled his chair. He froze watching her sit on his lap and wrap her arms around his neck. Normally he didn't mind a no strings hook-up with her, but it just felt weird with Ephra in his body too.

Callie leaned forward and kissed him deeply, thrusting her tongue in his mouth.

Forget the ley lines. Let's just use her blood.

The laughter escaped from him before he could control it.

Callie pulled back, confused. "Is my kissing humorous?"

"No, no, I'm sorry. A random thought popped into my mind. I didn't mean to laugh." He lifted her up and stood up. "But it's been a long day and we start again early tomorrow, so I'm going to call it a night."

Callie's bottom lip jutted out. "I can be quick. Don't you want me?" Her hand stroked down the center of her cleavage.

Is she a succubus?

Raine gave Callie a quick hug. "It really was good to see you. I'm sure I'll see you around soon."

He hightailed it out of there and rushed back to the room.

He changed into the shorts he slept in and flopped onto the center of the king-size bed.

So, you mate with her often?

It was so weird to have a conversation in an empty room. He had nothing better to do than stare up at the ceiling. "We're both single and sometimes we run into each other and relieve a little pressure. We are in no way actual mates." Callie was a sweet girl, but he couldn't see spending thousands of years with her.

You are too good for her. What kind of supernatural is she?

"She said she's fae, but I've never seen her wings or anything."

I don't trust her. But enough about her. Do you think you could look on your internet to see what happened to a family I used to know?

"Sure, there aren't a lot of sites that will have data from that far back, but let's see what we can do."

He grabbed his laptop and got comfortable on the couch. "Who am I looking for?"

Their family name was Alborn. They lived

in Yerba Buena. There was a father named Christopher, a son named James, and a daughter named Calliope.

Raine had a sinking feeling in his stomach. It didn't help that he could feel Ephra's anxiety. "Let me start with Yerba Buena, because I'm not familiar with that one."

A quick search explained that was the name of the San Francisco area back in the 1800s. He found a site with old census data and started combing the lists.

It took twenty minutes, but he found their records. "Here they are. Christopher died in 1823. James and Calliope both died in the 1880s."

He was proud of his find, but Ephra was silent.

"These weren't just people you knew, were they?"

I had met Christopher on one of my runs on this plane. It was love at first sight for both of us. The first couple of years I would come up, spend a couple of days, then go back down. When I found out I was pregnant with James,

I went to my superior and asked if I could live here.

"And how do the priests that hunted you come into this?"

I was allowed to live here, but I still had to collect souls. In my happiness, I had gotten complacent and walked right into a trap. They captured me and I guess figured out how to bind my soul. My sweet Calliope had the blondest curls and bright green eyes. James was so loveable and funny. That's why I was so desperate to get out of here. I needed to know what happened to them.

Raine felt like shit. He judged her without knowing anything about her. "Let me see if you have any descendants."

That would be wonderful. I'd love to meet my great-grandchildren.

He prayed he found someone. It took some internet sleuthing and a lot of social media searching, but he found an extensive family that still lived in the area. "You have a lot of family, actually. I'll keep searching for how to get a hold of them and as soon as the expo is over tomorrow, I promise I'll take you to see them."

Thank you, I know that's asking a lot from someone you just met.

"Cupids are all about love. Not just romantic love either. If I can reunite you with your family, I'll do everything in my power to do so."

I guess this means I can't make fun of you tomorrow.

It sounded good to hear her teasing again. He didn't want to walk around with a depressed demon inside him for the next two days.

Chapter Five

Raine stood in the middle of the makeshift archery field and aimed his arrow. Every shot he took was a perfect bulls-eye. They were stuck firmly in the target, not one bounced or fell out.

Several council members stood off to the side, watching and whispering. When the class was over, Guthrie waved him over. "It's quite the puzzle how you are so good here, but in the field, you have so little success."

Raine let out a deep sigh. "I don't understand either. I swear when I leave, the couples are happy and well connected."

"Now that we see for ourselves that you are

capable, I think we should give you one last chance. We'll send someone with you on your next mission. If they can attest to your skills, we'll decide what to do with you next."

"I understand. Thank you, sir."

Guthrie patted him on the shoulder and left.

They can see you are competent. You don't need a babysitter.

"I appreciate the vote of confidence, but I have to do everything they say if I want to stay a cupid."

Would it be so bad if you weren't?

Raine stared into the woods, contemplating her question. "It's all I've ever known. Every man in my family is a cupid."

Being a cupid is a job. What are you without that job?

When he had no response, she continued on.

Maybe you need to spend some time finding out what else you are. Until I met Christopher, I thought my entire existence would be collecting souls. He opened my eyes to all the possibilities there were out there.

"I'm sorry you didn't get to say goodbye to him. I can ask around, see if anyone is friends with any angels and see if they'll check on your family in heaven and make sure they are good?"

Do you think they were allowed in heaven? They did come from a demon.

Raine could hear the fear in her voice.

What if I doomed them to hell because I was selfish and tried to take more than was my due?

Raine wracked his brain with how to comfort her, but his phone alerted it was time for the next session.

Back to you. What's next?

She tried to sound chipper, but it was obviously fake.

"You're going to love this next one. We're going to learn about making chocolates. Sometimes we send mates gifts from the other to encourage the relationship. Obviously, we could just buy them, but the council is old-fashioned and wants us to be able to do everything on our own."

If we get to taste what we make, can I take over for a few minutes? I promise to give control back right after.

Holy shit, she actually asked permission. "I think that's fair."

He followed the stream of cupids heading into Skipper's restaurant. It wasn't open for lunch, so they turned it into makeshift kitchen stations.

The smell of chocolate permeated the air.

Oh, everything looks so good. Can I just have control now? You can talk me through anything I might mess up. I promise I won't embarrass you.

He chuckled quietly. "Okay, take my body." He hadn't meant for it to sound provocative, but given her laughter in his head, she definitely had taken it that way.

He hid the slight shiver as they switched roles. It was scary how easily he'd come to trust her.

Just do me a favor and when you get a taste of it, don't lick the bowl in front of all these people.

Chapter Six

"**L**ast class of the day, then I'll take you back to Skipper's for a steak dinner."

That sounds amazing. I ate so much chocolate I think I could fall asleep, but I don't know if I actually can sleep inside you.

"Something I never thought I'd have to contemplate."

He sat in the last row all the way against the wall. This was going to be an uncomfortable class, and he wanted to be able to escape if needed.

As he scrolled Facebook on his phone waiting for the class to start, two guys walked up. "It looks like you had the same idea as us.

Mind if we sit here?"

The room was almost completely full, so they didn't have many other options. "Sure, we can be uncomfortable together."

He sat down and held out his hand. "My name's Simon, and this is Finn."

Raine shook each of their hands. "Raine, nice to meet you."

You don't want to introduce me?

He ignored her laughter.

Is it just me or is everyone staring? The guy two rows up is turned around. Did I leave chocolate on your face?

A man walked down the aisle in front of them and scowled at Finn. "Not surprised to see you in this class, Deuce."

The name Deuce triggered a memory. He'd heard rumors about the cupid. Something about cheating. Raine didn't care much for gossip. He'd judge the guy on his own.

A tall cupid Raine vaguely recognized walked to the front and stood at the podium. "It's nice to see so many of you here. This is

'How not to fracture your soul' so if this isn't the class you wanted, I'll give you a few seconds to run."

Nervous laughter rippled across the crowd.

Your soul's fracture? How in the hell does love make your soul fracture?

He wanted to answer her, but he didn't want everyone around him thinking he was talking to himself.

The speaker paced across the stage as he spoke. "There is no more noble cause than bringing two mates together, but you have to understand the risk to you if the couple fails. How many of you have experienced a fracture already?"

Almost the entire room held up a hand.

"Decades ago, it was extremely rare for a cupid to have a fracture. Maybe it's the internet or just the culture moving away from monogamy, but it's becoming a bigger and bigger problem. I remember the first time I lost a piece of my soul. The pain was unlike anything I'd ever felt in my life. For days, I didn't want to go on. The depression that engulfed me was incredible and all-consuming. It took time and a few successful missions and eventually I managed to continue on with that little missing piece, always there like a splinter in your foot. I have four of these splinters as I call them. Always there, a faint pain."

Well, that all sounds terrible. It's not worth it. Let them find love on their own.

The cupid continued on. "Now let's talk about how we can prevent this."

***

I hope you took lots of notes. People think badly of demons, but nothing we do causes us torturous pain.

Raine didn't disagree with Ephra, but he also believed in the bigger picture and would risk every part of himself to bring two mates together.

Once the crowd had mostly filed out, he followed Finn and Simon out of the room.

Simon was pale and sweating. "I really don't

think I was ready for that class."

Raine thought he looked ready to throw up.

Finn rubbed his back. "Take deep breaths. He made it sound way worse than it actually is."

Raine stared at him with wide eyes. Why would he lie to this obviously new cupid?

He was shoved back as a man pushed past him and grabbed Finn's wrist. "What did you do to him? Why's he look like shit?"

Simon whimpered as he held a hand up. "Charles, stop, please. No one did anything to me. That class was a little intense, and I got overwhelmed."

Charles narrowed his eyes. "We'll talk about that part later. You've got a lot of explaining to do."

Finn jerked his hand free. "I suggest you step back."

Charles stepped closer.

Raine didn't know any of these people, but that didn't mean he could just let this new guy come in and start a fight. He tried stepping between them. "Why don't we all just take a breath."

Charles whipped an arm out and grabbed a handful of Raine's shirt. "When I'm done with him, I'll be happy to teach you a lesson."

Raine's body convulsed. "Oh shit." Ephra had taken over his body and she was pissed.

She grabbed his wrist and jerked his hand backward until they heard a pop. Her other hand came up and grabbed his neck. "I suggest you apologize to each of us then walk away or I promise you I can spend the rest of the night skinning you alive."

The blood drained from Charles' face. He mumbled his apologies and took off.

Damn, you're scary.

She looked over at the two remaining men. She wasn't sure which one looked more shocked, or maybe it was horrified. There was a small shiver as Ephra gave back control. Of course, she didn't want to do damage control. "I didn't mean any of that. I've just found if you come up with a scary enough threat, the bully tends to run off."

They nodded, but still looked unsure of him.

"Well, I guess we better be going. Have a good night." Finn waved at him and pulled Simon along with him.

Did I lose two new friends for you? I'm sorry. I saw red and reacted without thinking.

"It's okay. I was impressed. You were badass."

I could entertain you for days with the stories of what I've done.

"No, that's okay. Impressed doesn't mean I want details." His stomach soured just thinking about what she'd likely done.

If you change your mind, let me know. Now about that steak dinner.

"You have a one track mind." He chuckled as he made his way toward Skippers. "Let's get you a four course meal. You've earned it."

Can we make it five and finish with ice cream again? This time without someone trying to jump your bones.

Chapter Seven

Raine laid on the round chair, staring up at the stars. The roof was a garden oasis with plenty of private alcoves.

I realized I don't know anything about you. Callie wasn't your mate. Have you ever had one?

"No. I guess I've been so focused on other people that I didn't look for anyone for myself."

That sounds lonely. Always finding love for others, then going home to an empty house.

"Well, when you say it like that."

She chuckled softly.

"I probably would have had relationships,

but I've been struggling for so long with my couples not completing the connection that it's all I've thought about."

You said you come from a family of cupids. What do they think of your issues?

"I wouldn't know. I do everything I can to avoid them. I'm too ashamed to admit my failures. Every cupid in my family has had a near perfect record. Honestly, I was a legacy and expectations were high for me."

I'm sorry I gave you such a hard time in the beginning. I didn't realize how important this was.

"It's not all bad. I think my mom knows something is up. When she manages to pin me down, she makes sure to avoid all topics related to work."

Women can't be cupids, right? So what is she?

"Mom's a siren. Dad jokes she used her powers to trap him."

That is horrible.

"He's just kidding. He loves her with every

fiber of his being. Plus, I met the cupid who shot them so I know they are true mates."

Is there like an internet or something you can look at and see if you are going to be shot? Seems like that would be a good perk of the job.

"That would be nice, wouldn't it? But no, there's no database of future assignments. I'll be surprised as the next guy if I ever get shot."

He yawned and stretched. It had been a long day.

I miss my body. It was a good body. I had nice breasts and Christopher loved grabbing my ass.

"When you reconnect with your people, will they be able to get your same body back?"

No idea. This is all new to me. If they do manage to get me out of you, what happens if they can't put me in any body. Do I just become a floating spirit? Do I die and go to hell?

Raine hadn't thought about what was going to happen to her. One thing was for sure, she'd suffered enough. "If they can't put you back in a body, you are welcome to stay with me. It's kind of nice having a friend around who I don't have to clean up after or who hogs the bed."

Very noble of you, but I wouldn't do that to you. I want you to have your own happily ever after and this would be the weirdest throuple in history.

"Throuple? So you are listening during my classes." It had been an interesting session learning about tricks to connect three mates. It was explained the third mate was a lost love from a previous life. Good to know the fates try to give everyone a fair chance at a happy life.

For all the shit I gave you, you really do have a fascinating job. I've learned so much and tried to absorb all the new words you guys use. If I do get out of you and get to meet my family, I don't want to be some weird, ancient creeper.

"You are way too cool to be a creeper. They are going to love you, demon and all."

Such a flatterer. Did they teach you that in cupid school too?

"No way baby, that's all me and my glorious charm."

Uh oh, it's getting cramped in here. Your ego is taking up too much space.

"You got jokes now? I've got my own private peanut gallery in my head."

Awe come on, you're going to miss me when I'm gone.

He sobered immediately. She was right, he was going to miss her. How had he gotten so attached to her so fast? This was going to be an all new type of soul fracturing.

Chapter Eight

Raine waited in the hall. After the expo's closing remarks, Guthrie had asked him to stay behind.

The older cupid was the last to leave the conference room and made his way over to him. "I've got a cupid in Black Hollow Massachusetts who is in between assignments and said he'd be glad to come with you on your next mission. His name's Adrian. I'll get his contact info, and you can let him know when you have something."

"Black Hollow, I think a friend just mentioned that place. There's a woman named Seraphine, right? I'm actually waiting to hear back from her. Maybe I'll just go there and see both of them."

"No need, my dear. I've come to you."

A tiny woman appeared behind him with Merlin by her side. "I saw the pictures of your egg and thought I would come see it for myself."

Woah, the power coming off these two. Can you feel it?

Guthrie pinched his eyebrows together. "Egg?"

Raine shrugged. "Nothing related to my work." He turned back to Seraphine and Merlin. "I have the remnants in my room."

Seraphine tsked. "Oh, dear. It appears I'm too late. Lead the way to your room."

He would have preferred to bring the pile of dust down to them, but when two of the most powerful people in the world suggest something, you don't argue.

He led them to his room and pointed at a small plate with dust and pebbles on it. "I got as much up from the carpet as I could."

Merlin held the plate up and studied the dust. "Did you watch it hatch? What came out of it?"

Seraphine walked around Raine, looking him up and down. "I see it now. I could tell your aura was off, but I wasn't sure why. The creature is inside you, isn't it?"

I take offense to that. Tell her I have a name. Sheesh.

He smiled at the annoyance in her voice.

Seraphine paused and looked at his face. "Is it talking to you?"

Merlin sniffed the plate and drew back. "Is that sulfur?"

Raine let out a deep breath. It felt weird admitting what had been happening for the last couple of days. "I didn't actually see the egg hatch. I came too and found the pile of dust on the ground and a voice in my head talking to me. Her name is Ephra, and she is a demon."

Seraphine pointed to the couch. "Perhaps you should start from the beginning. Where did you find the egg?"

Raine pulled out the map he'd had with him on the hike and spread it out. "I had been hiking down the mountain. There was incessant whispering leading me to a cave."

And you just followed them? Who does that?

"Right, that's what I kept telling myself."

Seraphine and Merlin exchanged glances.

"Sorry, Ephra was giving me crap. Anyways, I went into the cave and found a box. Inside the box was this rock looking thing. I wanted to leave it, but the whispering kept insisting I take it, so I gave in. I figured with all the supes I know, someone would have an idea what it was."

Seraphine tapped her fingers on the arm of the couch for a few seconds. "Does Ephra know how she came to be trapped in the egg?"

He nodded. "She was living on this plane with her human husband and children and was found by priests. She isn't sure what they did. One minute she was being held by them, then the next she was inside me."

Merlin shook his head. "Terrible what they

used to do to people they didn't understand." He turned toward Seraphine. "So, how do we get her out?"

Raine held up a hand to get their attention. "If removing her causes her to die, then I've already told her she can stay with me."

They exchanged surprised looks.

Seraphine smiled widely. "That's very noble of you, but I don't think you have to take it that far." She turned back to Merlin. "If we could find where they disposed of her body, we should be able to put her back, right?"

"In theory, yes, but that was centuries ago. How do we find a random body?"

"The box the egg was in was made of bones."

What?

"What?"

"What?"

Three identical questions flew at him at the same time.

You didn't think to mention that to me before?

"This is my first disembodied soul, okay? I didn't think about it."

Merlin pushed the map toward him. "Point to where the cave is. I'll get the box and bring it back."

Raine drew a circle with his finger. "Somewhere around here."

Merlin got up and opened a portal. A few seconds later, the portal flashed back open, and he stepped through with the box.

Why didn't you bring that with you instead of just grabbing the egg?

"Do you see how creepy that thing is? I didn't want to get anywhere near it."

That's my body you are talking about. It's a good body, remember?

"Yes, I remember you have a good body." He rolled his eyes toward Seraphine and Merlin. "She's very upset I didn't bring the box the first time."

Seraphine had a twinkle in her eye. "You get along quite well, don't you?"

"The forced proximity didn't really allow for anything else. But yes, I think we're friends."

Awe, you called me your friend.

Seraphine and Merlin put their heads together, tossing out various ideas. "Sounds good." Seraphine grabbed her cell phone and made a phone call. "Hi, I need your help. I'll be there in a minute to get you."

She hung up and opened a portal. A few seconds later, she stepped back through with a large, intense looking guy.

Oh shit.

Seraphine pointed toward Raine. "This is King, he's one of the Princes of Hell."

Okay. Three powerful beings in his hotel room now. "Nice to meet you, sir."

King cocked his head to the side. "Ephra, there you are. We wondered what had happened to you."

Tell him I'm bowing to him.

"Um, she said to tell you she is bowing to you."

Merlin reached out and shook King's hand. "Good to see you again. So, we think between the three of us, we can pull her soul from him and put it back into her body." He held up the box of bones.

Raine interjected before he could finish. "But if pulling her out kills her, we don't want you to do it."

King snorted and shook his head. "She's got you hooked good. I promise if anything goes wrong and she gets sent down, I will personally bring her back."

Raine glanced at Seraphine.

She nodded gently. "You can trust him."

Raine stood up and nodded to each of them. "Okay, what do we do?"

Merlin led them to the bed and set the box down. "You lay on that side and just hold still. It might get a bit uncomfortable but hang on as long as you can."

You don't have to do this. I don't want you to get hurt.

He laid on the bed. "You deserve happiness too. We're doing this."

Raine tried to relax. Hard to do with the trio standing over him all whispering different things under their breath.

The box started to shake, then separated

and formed into the shape of a body.

Not weird at all to be lying next to a skeleton.

Merlin glanced at him. "Here we go."

Wind whipped through the room, the lights flashed on and off rapidly. Raine's entire body raged with heat. He was burning from the inside out. His roar of pain echoed throughout the room.

Raine, tell them to stop. Please don't do this to yourself.

Sweat, or maybe it was tears, poured down his face, then he blissfully passed out.

When he came to, it was dark outside, and no one stood over the bed any longer. His head whipped to the side. It was empty.

He bolted up. "Ephra, what happened to her?"

Merlin and Seraphine were sitting on the couch with a young blonde. She smiled shyly and waved to him. "Hi Raine."

He climbed off the bed and walked toward them on wobbly legs. "I can't believe it worked.

You're okay?"

Merlin and Seraphine stood up. "We're going to go. We wanted to make sure you woke up first." Seraphine held her hand out to him. "I heard Guthrie mention the cupid in Black Hollow. If you come visit, I hope you'll stop in and see me."

He nodded, then shook both their hands. "Thank you for everything."

They waved goodbye to Ephra and left the room.

She stood up and pinched the shirt she was wearing. "So when I came to, I was naked. I hope you don't mind me borrowing some clothes? Merlin said Jianna was going to send some clothes up."

"I can't believe you're really here. Is this the way you were when they took you? You're not missing any toes or anything?" He knew it was a weird question, but it really didn't look like there were 206 bones in the box.

She put her hands on her hips and turned from side to side. "I know it doesn't look like much in these clothes, but this is my body and, as promised, it's a good one."

He let out a breath and dragged his hands down his face. "This has been the most insane weekend."

They laughed awkwardly. Neither was sure what to do next. She stepped toward him and held her arms out. "Thank you for everything."

He pulled her into a hug and knew instantly this was his mate. He didn't need a cupid's arrow to shoot him.

She stepped back and brushed her hair over her shoulder, then gasped. "It's so nice to have hair again to do that."

He rubbed his smooth head. "I don't miss hair in the least." He glanced around the quiet room. "So, what now?"

"I say we get clothes and head to Lumberjacks. They have a buffet. I want to try all of it."

"You do have a couple of hundred years to make up for, don't you?"

A knock on the door interrupted them. He let in a bellhop rolling a cart with several outfits hung on it. "From Jianna and Merlin for all your troubles while you were here."

Raine grabbed his wallet and handed the kid a tip.

Ephra ran her hands along the silks and satins. "No offense, but these are much nicer than your clothes."

"I bet they are going to look a lot better on you than they would me."

She grabbed a lavender dress and a small bag. "I'll be right back."

He sat on the couch and laid his head back. He still couldn't believe everything that had happened in the last few days.

Through the bathroom door she called out to him. "I know you have stuff to do with the council, but is there any chance you can take a couple of days and help me find my family? I've learned a lot, but I'm not sure I'm ready for all that 2022 has to offer."

His shoulders visibly relaxed. He wasn't ready to say goodbye, but didn't have an excuse of his own. "I don't have an open assignment right now, so I'll be your chauffeur and tour guide until I do." He bit his lip, then decided to continue on. "You are welcome to come to Black Hollow with me too. It's supposed to be an incredible town full of supernaturals all living together."

"I would love that. I'd love the chance to thank Seraphine again for her help."

The door clicked open. His breath was taken from him. She glowed with happiness. She spun in a circle. "What do you think?"

"I think you look stunning." Her cheeks reddened. He hadn't expected her to be shy. He stood up and bowed slightly. "May I take you to an all you can eat buffet?"

She giggled as she took his hand. "You sure know your way to a girl's heart."

He held the door open for her. "What kind of cupid would I be if I didn't?"

She gasped. "I totally forgot. Can I meet you at Lumberjacks? There's something I need to do."

"Um, sure. I'll get us a table."

***

Raine sat at the table sipping water. Ephra had been gone for twenty minutes. He was worried she was trapped in an elevator or stuck in the bathroom and didn't know how to use the automatic toilet flusher.

He choked on his water as she came into view, dragging Callie by the upper arm. The other girl looked a mess, with her hair sticking up and her clothes twisted.

Ephra shoved her into a chair, then sat down.

He was at a loss.

Ephra elbowed Callie. "Come on."

Callie crossed her arms and huffed.

Ephra rolled her eyes and looked back at Raine. "There is absolutely nothing wrong with your cupid powers. Callie here has been stalking you for decades and undoing the couples after you leave."

His jaw fell open. "Wait, you're not fae, are you? You're an anti-cupid?"

Callie lurched forward and slapped the table. "I was one of the best, too. I was all set to be promoted to the highest level. My bosses came on assignment to evaluate me. I found you and your couple and undid your binding. Two days later, we check-in and they are back together. I undid the bind again, but when we checked in again, they were still together. My bosses lost confidence in me and demoted me."

"Wait, I remember that. It was New York City during the holidays. There was no reason to rush off. I had checked in on the couple too since I stayed in town and couldn't figure out why my shots weren't sticking. I kept redoing it and pushing them toward romantic interludes and sending flowers to her from him. I can't believe that was you."

She nodded emphatically. "After that, I made it my mission to get you demoted too. Any time I had a free moment, I would hunt you down and undo your work. I thought the cherry on top would be getting you to fall in love with me. You've been frustrating on that front."

Ephra snorted. "I guess you just weren't woman enough to close the deal." She reached over and grabbed Callie by the back of the neck. "You are going to go on your way and never come near Raine or any of his charges ever again. If I find out you did, I'll do all those things I promised you I would do when I found you in the casino."

Callie's face paled. She jerked free and took off.

After hearing Ephra's threat to the jackass the day before, he could only imagine what she said to Callie.

Ephra took a deep breath and smiled at Raine. "Ready to eat?"

He reached forward and grabbed her hand. He placed a kiss on the top of her hand. "You're incredible. I'm so thankful I hatched you." There was a brief pause, then they burst into laughter. "I guess I could have said that better. Let's go get our eat on."

Chapter Nine

Raine carried Ephra's new luggage down to the lobby. Thanks to Jianna, she had everything she would need for the next few days. As soon as they were on the road to find Ephra's family, he'd stop at a mall and take her shopping.

On the way out the door, he remembered the woman he'd met when he'd checked in. "Hang on, I have an idea."

They waited in the check-in line. When it was their turn, he waved the person behind him to go ahead. "We're waiting for someone specific. You can go first."

When the person he wanted called next, he

led Ephra to the counter.

"Did you need something before checking out?"

Raine paused for a second. He really didn't know how his request was going to go over. For Ephra, he'd take the risk. "Hi Velvet, if I'm not mistaken I believe you are an Angel?"

The blonde smiled sweetly. "You would be correct."

Out of the corner of his eye, he saw Ephra smile excitedly.

"I don't know what the protocols are on all this, so don't like smite me or anything. This is Ephra. She's been trapped in a cave for 200 years."

Velvet gasped. "Everyone's been talking about that. Merlin helped set you right last night, didn't he?"

Ephra nodded. "I'm so thankful to him for that and to Jianna for giving me some outfits so I didn't have to walk around in his gym clothes."

Raine thought she looked cute in his oversized clothes. "Anyway, she had a family back then, and she'd really like confirmation they made it to heaven and are okay. Is that something you could check for her?"

Velvet turned and waved to get the attention of the guy next to her. "I need to take a quick break. I'll be back."

She didn't wait for permission. She waved at them to follow her. "There's a couple of small private offices back here. Jianna won't mind if we use one."

The room she led them to was plain except for a table and four chairs and a small fridge in the corner. She handed them each a bottle of water and waved at them to sit. "Give me a few minutes and I'll be back." She blinked out of view.

"Well, that's a new one for me." Raine had never met an angel, let alone know how their magic worked.

"Me too, but then again, most things are." Ephra chuckled, then started chewing on her nail.

Raine grabbed her hand and squeezed. "It's going to be fine. Take a deep breath."

On her third deep breath, Velvet reappeared in the room. "I have good news. Your family is safe and sound in heaven. Would you like to see?"

Ephra's jaw dropped. "I can go see them?"

"Not exactly. I can show you a glimpse of them, almost like you'd be watching a movie."

Ephra leaned forward excitedly. "Please, I'll take anything I can get."

Velvet waved her hand, and an image of a lake appeared on the wall. A man walked into view, waving to several people picnicking on the water's edge.

Ephra ran to the wall and reached up to touch Christopher. "He looks just like he did the last time I saw him. I thought he had lived a long life?"

"In Heaven, they can choose what age they want to be. Most people don't choose their older selves."

A man and a woman got up and hugged Christopher.

Ephra gasped. "Is that James and Calliope?"

Raine couldn't imagine how she felt seeing her children all grown up, and she had missed it.

"Those are your children and around them are their spouses and children. These are your descendants."

Ephra collapsed on the floor sobbing.

Velvet walked over and held out her hand. "There's nothing to be sad about."

Ephra let the angel wrap her in a hug. "I'm not sad, I'm relieved. I had been so worried they'd be in Hell since they came from me."

"They were judged for who they were and you made very special people. They are exactly where they should be."

Ephra stepped out of the embrace and wiped her face dry. "Thank you for this. I'll be eternally grateful."

Velvet shrugged as she led them to the door. "Happy to help and honestly, the resort owes you since they didn't find your egg when they were first building the place. Jianna thinks it's because you weren't meant to be found until Raine arrived."

Ephra glanced at him shyly. He knew she was his mate, but it wasn't something they'd talked about. They hadn't even kissed yet. Would she be okay with the angel's insinuation that they were meant to be together?

Velvet waved to them as she went back to the registration desk.

Raine led the way outside and asked the valet for a car to take them into town. They were going to rent a car and go on a road trip to meet her living family. "Are you okay?"

Ephra nodded eagerly. "Thank you so much for risking being smited for me. I owe you so much for everything you've done for me."

"I think we're even. You figured out Callie was behind my work problems, and now I should be good to go."

Ephra bit her lip for a second. "I kind of like the idea that I might have been hidden away, waiting for you."

"Me too." For all the ways there was to meet your mate, this might be the best. Who else can say they were love possessed?

Epilogue

Three weeks later

"So this is Black Hollow." Ephra leaned against the passenger window and waved at everyone they drove past.

Raine whistled as he took in the names of the businesses. "They are seriously quirky here, aren't they?" He pulled the car up in front of the Daydreamer Inn. "Looks like we have a welcoming committee."

Seraphine led a man down the steps and met them at their car. Ephra jumped out and hugged the older woman. "It's so good to see you again. Thank you again for saving me. I'll never be able to repay you."

Seraphine waved her off. "Please dear, I will always help someone in need."

The man with her held his hand out to Raine. "Hey, I'm Adrian Lovejoy. I guess I'm going to shadow your next mission. Although I heard about that anti-cupid, so it sounds like this is just a formality."

Raine still felt relief every time he thought about Ephra catching Callie for him. "I'm confident it will go well but also scared it won't, so I'll take the company and extra set of eyes."

A blonde man stumbled through the tree line and ignored them as he staggered his way toward town.

Raine cocked his head as he watched the stranger. "Is that... no, it can't be."

Adrian nodded sadly. "Yep, that's Tanner James. He's been like that since being stripped of his cupid powers."

"Why'd he lose them?" Ephra stared sadly toward the man as he disappeared down the road.

"He was sleeping with his charges before shooting them with arrows."

Seraphine tsked. "It's water under the bridge and I have a feeling things are going to be turning around for him very soon."

Raine hoped so. As close as he had come to losing his powers, he could imagine what the other disgraced cupid was going through.

Seraphine cleared her throat and gave them a bright smile. "Enough of that. I want to give you a tour of Black Hollow and all it has to offer."

Raine had thought it was only a work trip, but maybe Seraphine had hoped for more. Every day he spent with Ephra was one day closer to when he'd ask her to marry him. Maybe settling down in a town full of paranormals was exactly what they needed.

The End

If you're intrigued by Tanner James, you'll want to check out Black Hollow: Forgiving Love coming March 2022.

Want more Crimson Moon Hideaway Stories?
Join the Fan Page to stay up to date on the
latest releases:
https://www.facebook.com/groups/8050373
03324967

ABOUT THE AUTHOR

Cassidy is a born and raised Floridian who loves to travel but never forgets where her roots are. She married her high school sweetheart and has three kids and one rescue dog she probably loves more than her kids. She love's all things Ireland and has been lucky enough to visit twice. Her dream is to watch a baseball game in every MLB stadium in the country.

To learn more about Cassidy please visit her online at www.cassidykoconnor.com.

You can also find her on Facebook at www.facebook.com/cassidykoconnorauthor

She always welcomes new friends and encourages readers to reach out to her.

Other Books by the Author

Raven's Haven Series
Fighting For Forgiveness

Sassy Mates: In My Mate's Sight

Sassy Mates: In My Mate's Defense

Paranormal Dating Agency: My Oath To You

Stand Alones
Broken Dreams

The Laird's Promise

Sexy In White

Forever Yours, Casey

To Steal a Prince's Heart

Wicked Wonderland Retreat Box Set

Her Royal Choice: A Reverse Harem Romance

The Love's Protector Series
Tempted by the Fae

Seduced by the Fae

Charmed by the Fae

Healed by the Fae

Redeemed by the Fae

Black Hollow Series

Reviving Love

Sacrificing Love

Accepting Love

Resisting Love

Mending Love

The Nightshade Guild

All twelve mages of the Nightshade Guild have lost their powers! Read each of their stories to find out how they get their powers back and be sure not to miss the final book of the year, when the mages come together to defeat whoever is behind it all!

Magic Mishap by Lily Winter

Releases January 27, 2022, with featured mage Luna Graves

Magic Confined by Mandy Rosko

Releases February 24, 2022, with featured Mage: Lisa Chen

Magic Clouded by Renee Hewett
Releases March 24, 2022, with featured mage
Sunny Burson

Magic Mayhem by Louisa Bacio
Releases April 28, 2022, with featured mage
Serena Moon

Magic Mourning by Cherron Riser
Releases May 26, 2022, with featured mage
Charlotte "Charlie" Nocker

Magic Flawed by Jennifer Wedmore
Releases June 23, 2022, with featured mage
Morwen Rowe

Magic Deadfall by Gracen Miller
Releases July 28, 2022, with featured mage
Nicoletta "Nic" Dean

Magic Exposed by Lia Davis
Releases August 25, 2022, with featured mage
Jemma Blackwood

Magic Reflected by Sheri Lyn
Releases September 22, 2022, with featured
mage Cale Cawthorn

Magic Masque by Kerry Adrienne

*Releases October 27, 2022, with featured mage
Arion*

Magic Malfunction by Abigail Kade

*Releases November 30, 2022, with featured
mage Finnegan Padrick*

Magic Burned by Cassidy K. O'Connor

*Releases December 29, 2022, with featured mage
Isla Ryan*

The Nightshade Guild

Year One:

Guarding Ameria

Mated to a Mage by Cassidy K. O'Connor

Featured Mage: Isla Ryan

Mage you Blink by Gracen Miller

Featured Mage: Nicoletta "Nic" Dean

Mage You Look by Abigail Kade

Featured Mage: Finnegan Padrick

Shadow Mage by Lia Davis

Featured Mage: Jemma Blackwood

Mage Crafted by Cherron Riser

Featured Mage: Charlotte "Charlie" Nocker

Mage of Misfortune by Lily Winter

Featured Mage: Luna Graves

Mage in Hell by Sheri Lyn

Featured Mage: Cale Cawthorn

Sunny Mage by Renee Hewett

Featured Mage: Sunny Burson

Half-Blood Mage by Landra Graf

Featured Mage: Demi Mephisto

Sea Mage by Louisa Bacio

Featured Mage: Serena Moon

You Mage Me by Jennifer Wedmore

Featured Mage: Morwen Rowe

Midwinter Mage by Kerry Adrienne

Featured Mage: Arion